A TREE COULD BE

Natalia,
Grow tall as the trees! ☺

WRITTEN & ILLUSTRATED BY
GINA STEVENS

FOR GRIFFIN

AFTER GETTING LOST IN THE WOODS,
I HOPE YOU ALWAYS COME HOME WITH MESSY HAIR,
DIRTY FEET AND A *full heart*.

LOVE, MOM

Nine18 Creative LLC

Nine18Creative@gmail.com

www.Nine18creative.com

Text and illustrations copyright © 2020 by Gina Stevens

Third Edition - 2024

Printed in the United States of America

ISBN 978-1-7347231-0-6 (Hardcover)

One October, a young boy named Griffin
wandered into the woods to explore.
He even brought along his dog Roscoe
who'd been on this path before.

Each time they hiked,
          they found treasures — big and small.
     And today they noticed something —
GIGANTIC trees standing tall!

He thought the trees looked familiar,
          yet *different* somehow.
All the leaves' colors so splendid
          he said to himself,

          ...HOLY COW!

Griffin walked down the trail
and spotted — then climbed — a big birch tree.
With that great BIRD'S-EYE VIEW, it showed him
just how *different* all the trees could be.

Many were green with sharp pointy needles,
some branches ideal for a fort.
"SO MANY!" he thought with amazement,

Griffin hiked up the hillside,
and found a leaf he did
not recognize.

Quickly he opened his colorful tree guide
to study its **SHAPE**, **HUE**, and **SIZE**.

"A RED MAPLE!" he shouted in triumph,
then slid the leaf into his book.

"I'll reserach it later," he thought —
"when there's time for a much closer look."

Now, the wind could have carried that leaf
FROM A TREE LIVING MILES AWAY.

Leaves were flying all over,
like *sprinkles* atop a *sundae*.

Griffin and Roscoe continued their walk,
their feet crunched twigs on the path.
The gusty, cold air made them shiver,
raining leaves in its aftermath.

A squirrel ran up a tree trunk and
Griffin noticed the shape of its tail.
It looked like his kite stuck in the tree
after the wind made it set sail.

"IT'S TREE ART!" He whispered to Roscoe,
"FOR BIRDS AND BUGS TO ENJOY!"
His *heart skipped a beat* and he smiled
about the way he shared his old toy.

Then, as Griffin continued his journey,
his mind began to roam.
He remembered a hike last summer,
when the woods first felt like *home*.

The Redwood forest was lofty,
its trees the **tallest** he'd ever seen.
He pictured his family by the fire,
cooking meals with a log from the stream.

They had backpacked deep in the forest,
studying the trees of the West.
And when they felt they were tired,
they laid in their hammock to rest.

"We'll take **NOTHING BUT PICTURES**," Dad taught him.
"and leave nothing but **FOOTPRINTS** in sight."

And young Griffin took his dad's words to *heart*,
as critters hid and birds took *flight*.

Roscoe nudged his fingers
which made him reminisce even more.
Last winter, they'd hiked this same path
when the snow covered the forest floor.

Each December, he and his family
would bring a piece of the forest inside.
A tall Douglas fir they cut down to bring home;
Decorations they would hang with great pride.

While EVERGREENS keep their GREEN color,
DECIDUOUS TREES become BROWN.

And because they're all stunning, Griffin hopes

to REPLACE ALL THE TREES THEY'D CUT DOWN.

As the sky turned a deep blue,
Griffin saw a tree stump ahead.
He started off counting the rings,
amazed they could be so widespread.

He reached thirty-three —
a sizeable number, indeed.
So, he figured this tree must be FIVE TIMES his age,
after STARTING AS ONLY A SEED!

He opened his trusty tree guide
to study the **big blue spruce tree.**
It's not always blue, the guide said,
but it grows a foot per year, very slowly.

Once its *spruce cones* have fallen,
the sun and the rain make them sprout.
If you see the old leaves decaying—
don't be sad!
They *nourish* the soil to help out.

Roscoe shook when it started to sprinkle so they hid under a big tree.

"WHAT A GREAT CANOPY," he thought, "UMBRELLAS ARE WHAT TREES CAN BE!"

When the wind and the storms are most brutal,
the more **strongly** the roots will take hold.
So, a tree might not really be fragile;
It could be that its limbs are just old.

Griffin heard all the nature around him:

Bugs BUZZING and CROAKING frogs.

He could hear woodpeckers PECKING

while it rained, pouring CATS AND DOGS.

He checked his tree guide again while it rained,
just to see what new things he could learn.

"SWEET PECANS, SYRUP, OLIVES — all coming from trees!"
He was *fascinated* by each page he turned.

Griffin and Roscoe continued walking
after the skies started to clear.
Oops! He stumbled on a tree root.
"I Don't remember that being here!"

He imagined the roots were rippled,
cascading beneath the tree.
Could they stretch to the opposite side of the world?
That tree is **quite mighty**, you see.

He stopped and took a deep breath,
he had an important message to give:

"WE HAVE ALL THESE **GREAT TREES** TO PROTECT US,
GIVING OXYGEN, HELPING US LIVE!"

"Gosh, what would it feel like with no trees at all?

With no treehouse to play in, no leaves in the fall?

So, if not for the trees, do you know where we'd be?
With no jungle for George, and no forests to see!"

Just the thought of no trees could bring pain and despair,

yet, Griffin knew not to worry —

HIS TREES WERE STILL THERE!

When he saw the sun setting,
young Griffin made it home —
and climbed onto his swing near the bees' honeycomb.
As he swung, he looked at his house — it was **MADE OF TREES**, too!
Like big Lincoln Logs, built with some nails and some glue.

When he reached his front door, Griffin looked at the sky —
    the light was beginning to fade.
        He *loved* how the sunset colored the clouds,
but the oak tree was **darkened by shade.**

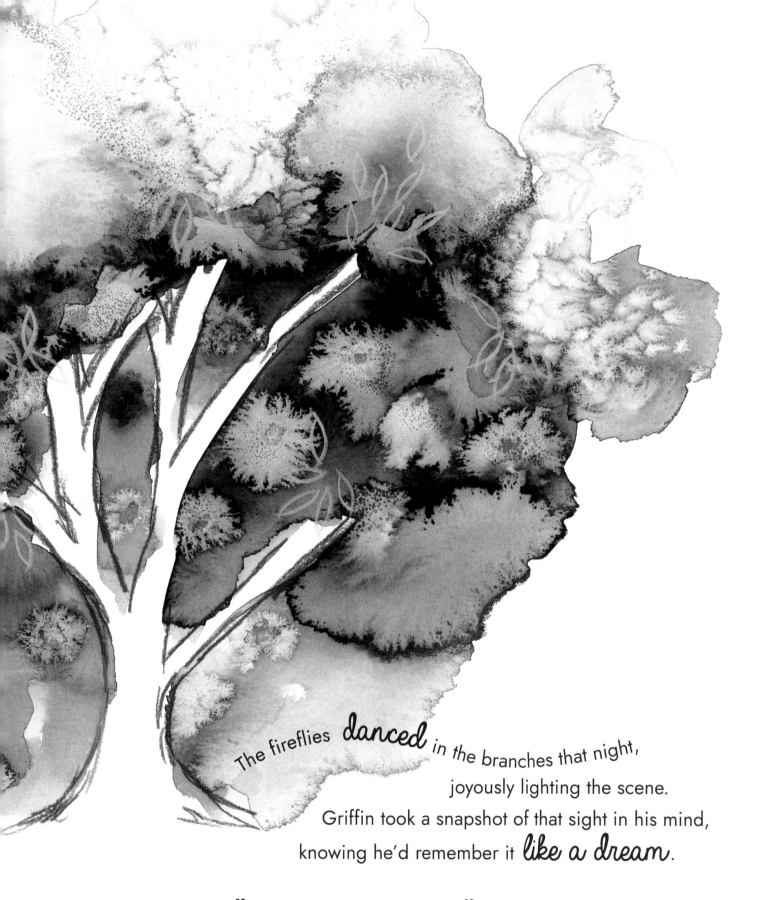

The fireflies *danced* in the branches that night,
joyously lighting the scene.
Griffin took a snapshot of that sight in his mind,
knowing he'd remember it *like a dream*.

Then, **"BEDTIME FOR YOU!"** called his mother.
He thought of the treasures he'd gathered that day —
acorns in one hand, an apple in the other.

When the full harvest moon starting *shining*
soon both Griffin and Roscoe would sleep.
Although Roscoe had counted his chipmunks,
COUNTING TREES had put Griffin to sleep!

As he dreamed, he could spy a whole forest,
with its plants and its creatures amuck,
who, by living together in tandem,
had created a scene of *great luck*.

Early the next morning,
when the sun took its place in the sky,
Griffin woke up *smiling* —
he had an idea to try.

"MOM! I WANT TO PLANT A FOREST RIGHT HERE IN OUR YARD!
I'LL GET FRESH DIRT AND A SHOVEL. IT CAN'T BE THAT HARD!"

He ran out the back door after breakfast
with acorns, a twig and string.
One of the most *beautiful days* ever was beginning!
He felt ready for what it would bring.

He started with the acorns,
        planting them row after row.
When he'd finished his work, he was *beaming* —
        now quite eager to watch his seeds grow.

        He called his mom over to see it.
                First **she hugged him**, then gazed at the seedlings.
        "YOU DID A WONDERFUL JOB," she said, smiling.
                        "I CAN SEE IT BY THE DIRT ON YOUR **KNEES**."

Griffin predicted the trees would be sturdy,
and he hoped they'd live to one-hundred and three.
Then he thought again, about all the things

A TREE COULD BE.

GINA STEVENS
Author & Illustrator

Gina sees life through a child's eyes and the lens of a polaroid.

So, it was only a matter of time before her passions for art, nature and raising children collided to produce her first book, *A Tree Could Be*.

Something is always growing in Gina's world. Plants in her sprawling garden. Her son. Her own design business, Nine18 Creative. In the rare moments she gets to herself, you'll find her barefoot probably trying to grow some exotic plant from a seed. Also, not running.

An artist to the core, she earned a degree in Fine Art — Graphic Design from Western Michigan University, then spent six years in corporate communications at Kellogg Company. She and her husband share their log home in Michigan with their son, two daughters and cat.

Check out Gina's other book:

Available at
www.Nine18creative.com